# A Summertime Song

Other books by Irene Haas

The Maggie B.
The Little Moon Theater

(Margaret K. McElderry Books)

# A Summertime Song

## BY IRENE HAAS

•

Margaret K. McElderry Books

**MARGARET K. McELDERRY BOOKS**
25 YEARS • 1972–1997

Margaret K. McElderry Books
An imprint of Simon & Schuster Children's Publishing Division
1230 Avenue of the Americas
New York, NY 10020

Book design by Irene Haas and Ann Bobco
The text of this book is set in Deepdene.
The illustrations are rendered in watercolor with some pastel.

Printed and bound in the United States of America
First Edition

10 9 8 7 6 5 4

Library of Congress Cataloging-in-Publication Data
Haas, Irene.
A summertime song / written and illustrated by Irene Haas.—1st ed.
p.    cm.
Summary: Lucy attends a magical birthday party and finds the doll
her grandmother loved and lost when she was a girl.
ISBN 0-689-50549-3
[1. Parties—Fiction. 2. Birthdays—Fiction. 3. Dolls—Fiction.
4. Grandmothers—Fiction. 5. Animals—Fiction.] I. Title.
PZ7.H1128Su    1997
[E]—dc20
96-17156    CIP    AP

For Marie-Charlotte

One warm summer night
Lucy opened her window
and in jumped a frog.
The frog gave Lucy an invitation to a birthday party
and a magic paper party hat to wear.
Then he jumped out again
into the garden.

Lucy put on the magic hat.
She went outside.
A finger of moonlight touched the hat and
FOOF!
Lucy was as little as a leaf.
Bugs and beetles all around were big as puppies,
and her grandma's lighted window
seemed as high up as the sky.

A taxi drove out of the shadows.
Lucy said to the driver,
"Take me to the birthday party, please!"
She settled down in the soft backseat,
and the taxi drove off into the nighttime garden.
"Good-bye, Grandma!" Lucy called. "Good-bye!"

As they traveled along,
Lucy looked at the driver's small fuzzy head.
"Baby Bird, why don't you fly?" she asked him.
"I'm too scared to try," he answered.
"What I like to do best is stay in my nest."
Then he tried to whistle a tune.

Soon, up ahead, they spied a mouse
rushing rushing to the party,
holding tight to her hat as she ran.
She cried, "Zut! I am late!
My husband would not wait
while I made my new chapeau
to wear to the fete!"
She stopped then and asked,
"Do you like it?"

Lucy vowed that she loved the new hat
and invited Madame Mouse
to join them in the taxi.

A little further on
they met an inchworm
slowly slowly inching to the party.
When he saw the taxi,
he stood on his tail and announced,
"I inch while I sleep,
I inch while I wake,
I inch until
my little feet ache.
But I don't care
how long I take,
I want a piece
of BIRTHDAY cake!"
So Lucy asked him to come along too
and they all continued the journey.

Baby Bird stopped the taxi one more time.
Standing alone in a patch of moonlight
was a tiny tattered old doll.
The doll bowed to them.
"Will my story have a happy ending?" he asked.
Lucy begged him please to tell his story
and he began.
"She lost me in the flowers
one summer night,
lost me in the shadows of pale moonlight.
So many lonely years have passed,
will my little friend find me
now at last?"
Lucy bowed to the doll,
took his tiny hand,
and invited him into the taxi too.

On they drove through the darkness,
chatting a bit, getting to be friends, when
all at once —BOOM!—
they bumped into something enormous!
A huge fat owl
looked down at them and howled,
"YUM YUM!
MY DINNER!"

Lucy sat still
and asked herself,
"Can this be real?
Will we be Owl's evening meal?"
Then it suddenly began to rain.
As Owl turned
to open his huge umbrella,
Baby Bird ZOOMED the taxi away!
They cheered three cheers for Baby Bird,
"HOORAY—HOORAY—HOORAY!"

At last they came to a big puddle.
The rain had stopped.
Little lights glittered on the far shore
and party music floated in the air.
One by one they each set sail
over the velvety water—
Lucy, Baby Bird, Madame Mouse,
Inchworm, and the doll.

Everyone from the garden was at the party!
Crickets sang summertime songs,
caterpillar clowns
served sweet tips of clover,
and there was dancing.

Then the music stopped and the lights went off.
In came—
the BIRTHDAY CAKE!
and just as the birthday song began there was a—
CRASH!
Out of the dark came Owl!
"YUM YUM!" he howled,
"MY DINNER!"
and he opened his beak to eat everybody up.

But the birthday song continued—
"Happy Birthday to you,
Happy Birthday to you,
Happy Birthday dear Owl—
Happy Birthday to you!"
"Oh," cried Owl, "You remembered. How kind!
Tonight I'll eat cake—not bugs.
Do you mind?"
Then he blew out the candles,
ate a big piece of cake,
and the party went merrily on.

When Inchworm ate some birthday cake
he turned into a handsome young moth.
"No more inching!" he cried,
and he taught Baby Bird to fly too.

And when Lucy offered Madame Mouse twenty gumdrops
to make a chapeau for her cat,
Mr. Mouse was astonished.
"Twenty gumdrops just for a HAT!" he exclaimed.

Now the moon was high.
The party was over.
Owl, asleep in a flower pot,
snored like faraway thunder.
Lucy bowed to the doll and told him,
"It's time for a happy ending!"

Baby Bird flew Lucy and the doll
up through the night
right into Grandma's window.

Grandma was sitting at her piano,
singing her sad old song.
"When I was a little girl,
he was my one and only.
He played with me, he stayed with me,
so I was never lonely. But—
I lost him in the flowers one summer night,
lost him in the shadows of pale moonlight—"

Lucy pulled off the magic paper party hat.
FOOF!
She was as big as before.
She tapped her grandma on the shoulder
and handed her the doll.

"Lucy—you FOUND him!" cried Grandma,
and turning back to the piano she sang,
"Lucy, Lucy, take a bow—
our song has a happy ending now!"

Then came bowls of strawberry ice cream,
and a hundred hugs and kisses,
and down in the garden
all night long
crickets sang
a summertime song.